Animal Music

HARRIET ZIEFERT

Illustrated by Donald Saaf

Walter Lorraine  Books

HOUGHTON MIFFLIN COMPANY BOSTON
1999

For Jamie and Will and their jazzy band
—H.M.Z.

To my musician friends, little and big,
and for Olaf and Isak
—D.S.

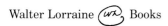

Walter Lorraine Books

Text copyright © 1999 by Harriet Ziefert
Illustrations copyright © 1999 by Donald Saaf

Library of Congress Cataloging-in-Publication Data
Ziefert, Harriet
   Animal Music / by Harriet Ziefert; illustrated by
Donald Saaf.
      p.   cm.
   Summary: An assortment of animals playing various instruments
make different kinds of music.
   ISBN 0-395-95294-8
   [1. Bands (Music)—Fiction.   2. Animals—Fiction.   3. Stories
in rhyme.]   I. Saaf, Donald, ill.   II. Title
PZ8.3.S114An   1999
[E]—dc21
                                                          98-32130
                                                             CIP
                                                              AC

Printed in China for Harriet Ziefert, Inc.
HZ1 10 9 8 7 6 5 4 3 2 1

Mr. Lion's Marching Band

The elephant thumps the big bass drum.
A-boom-a-boom...a-dum-a-dum!

The monkey taps the little snare drum.
Rat-a-tat-tat...rum-a-tee-tum!

Here comes the clarinet down the street.
Music and feet...music and feet.

Here comes the trumpet down the street.
Music and feet…music and feet.

The tuba is coming down the road.

Move out of the way, you silly toad!

They're playing loud;
They're marching fast.
Let's hurry and see them
Before they've passed.

Music and feet…
Music and feet.
I know a march
By the sound and the beat.

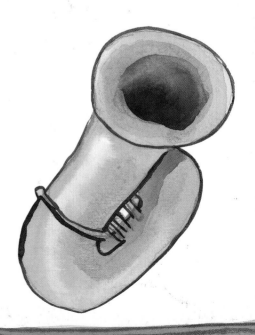

Mr. Lion is handsome and proud.
He leads the band in front of the crowd.

When I grow up, it would be grand,
If I could be leader of the band.

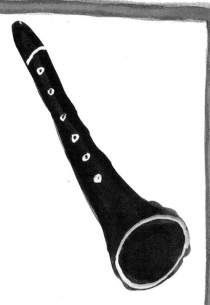

Around Mr. Lion
The animals play
Marching music.
It's a happy day!

Monkey and tiger,
Zebra and bear,
The best band ever
Heard anywhere.

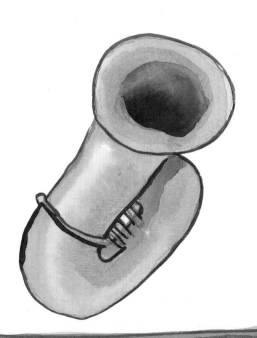

A-rum-a-tee...

Rum-a-tee...

RUM-A-TEE-

TUM!

Sheep's Dance Band

Dog plays piano,
Pig plays drum.

Mama Mouse claps
And starts to hum.

Goose plays mandolin,
Cow plays bass.

Animals dance
All over the place.

Goat plays banjo,
Cat plays fiddle.

All the dancers
Crowd to the middle.

The chicken plays
On a little kazoo.
The rooster sings...
Cock-a-doodle-doo!

Chicken and rooster
Tap the floor.
Everybody shouts,
We want more!

The cats are swinging,
The ducks look fine.

The late-comers all
Stand in line.

Grab a partner,
Little or big.

Dance to the music
Jiggety jig!

The band is playing
Nice and fast.
Hear this song,
It's the very last.

Swing your partner,
Feel the beat.
Sheep's Dance Band
Sure is sweet!

The music's over,
Off they go.
In their old red truck
To the next big show.